Have your own "great adventure".

Maryjane Zodtner

Dedicated by GG with much love to my great grandchildren:
Cal - Posey - Brooks - Ozzie

NOTHING, SOMETHING and ALL by Marajeane Zodtner
Illustrations and cover design by Madeleine Kunda

Lizard Head Publishing
319 Adams Ranch Road 1102
Telluride, CO 81435

www.lizardheadpublishing.com

ISBN 978-1-7355960-7-5

Printed in the U.S.A.

NOTHING, SOMETHING and ALL

Written by Marajeane Zodtner

Illustrated by Madeleine Kunda

On a sunny summer morning in the village of ALL, Jilly and Lil-Bro sat on their front steps thinking about what to do.

"Lil-Bro," said Jilly, "thinking of what to do is hard work. Let's walk into the village and then decide on our Great Adventure."

"FUN!" said Lil-Bro.

So off they went, hand in hand down the road into the village of ALL. Now, living in ALL was incredibly special because everyone who lived there had ALL they wanted . . .

ALL the time . . .

They had ALL the candy,
ALL the toys,
ALL the hugs and kisses,
and ALL the other good things you can imagine!

As the two children stood in the center of the village, Lil-Bro pointed to the road that went up . . . and up . . . and over the tallest hill in the valley.

"UP!" said Lil-Bro.

"Yes," said Jilly, as they started off. "That would be a real adventure."

When Jilly and Lil-Bro reached the top of the hill, they sat down to rest. They looked out over the valley and saw a new village, but it looked quite different from the village of ALL. These houses were run down, the trees and gardens were in sad shape, the children had no toys, and there was no joy or laughter to be heard.

"Why," said Jilly, "this village has nothing! Let's go find out where we are Lil-Bro." So hand in hand they the set off toward the village. As they arrived, a group of children came out to meet them.

"Hello," said Jilly, "I'm Jilly and this is my brother, Lil-Bro. We are from the village of ALL on the other side of the hill. What is the name of your village?"

A small boy, younger than Jilly, stepped forward and said, "This is the village of NOTHING because we have nothing most of the time. My name is Billy, and these are my friends. Will you stay and play with us?"

"Nice to meet you," said Jilly. "We've been looking for a Great Adventure. We are sorry to hear your story of NOTHING. It is getting late and we must walk back home now, but we will come and play with you another day."

Jilly and Lil-Bro returned over the hill to ALL and agreed that it had been a most interesting day, even if it had not been a Great Adventure.

The following day, Jilly and Lil-Bro were back on the front steps thinking.

"Where shall we go today Lil-Bro?" asked Jilly.

"WAGON!" said Lil-Bro.

"Do you want me to pull you on the road along the creek?" Jilly asked.

"YES!" Lil-Bro nodded happily.

So off they went along the road to the bridge at the end of the valley.

As they crossed the bridge Jilly said, "This must be a new way to the other part of our valley. What do you think we might find there today Lil-Bro?"

"SURPRISE!" said Lil-Bro.

As they came around the first bend in the road, they saw a large building with a sign that said, "Village of SOMETHING."

"Whatever does that mean, I wonder," whispered Jilly to Lil-Bro. She had barely stopped speaking when a large man in a red jacket with shiny brass buttons came out of the door and waved at them . . .

"Hello!" he said. "Welcome to SOMETHING, where everyone has a bit of something, even if it's not ALL or EVERYTHING."

"That's interesting." said Jilly. "Does that mean if I ask for something, I will get it?"

"No," said the man. "It means we have SOMETHING, and we need to be careful what we do with it so we don't end up with NOTHING."

"Oh I know about NOTHING," Jilly replied. "It looks like your village is doing much better than they are, since you must have SOMETHING in your pockets."

"Yes," said the big man, "we are incredibly happy here, and SOMETHING is always happening one way or another."

"I'll tell Mother and Father about your village, but we need to be on our way back to ALL now. We will come back soon to visit because we always need SOMETHING." said Jilly.

As they crossed the bridge back toward the village of ALL, Jilly asked Lil-Bro what he thought about the day's adventure.

"BETTER!" said Lil-Bro.

Yes, Jilly thought. SOMETHING is better than NOTHING.

The next morning at breakfast, Jilly told Mother and Father what they had found on their adventures. Then Jilly said,

"Lil-Bro, we need to help the families in the Village of NOTHING. Do you have any more good ideas?"

Lil-Bro closed his eyes and thought . . . and thought . . . and thought. Then he opened his eyes and smiled a big smile.

"SHARE!" said Lil-Bro.

"Yes! Yes!" said Jilly, jumping up and down. "We can SHARE, then every village will have SOMETHING. That makes it better in NOTHING, and we don't need everything in ALL. We better get started on our new adventure."

"That's a good idea!" said Mother and Father. "We will help too."

Quickly Jilly and Lil-Bro filled the red wagon up with toys, candy and books–everything they could manage. Then Jilly pulled the wagon, loaded with supplies (and with Lil-Bro) up and over the hill to NOTHING. Mother and Father followed them in their car filled with food, clothing, tools and materials of all sorts.

Many new friendships were made that day as the villagers took part in the happiness of sharing.

That night, as Mother and Father
tucked the children into bed,
Jilly whispered to Lil-Bro,

"Lil-Bro, sharing is a wonderful thing. It's better that everyone has SOMETHING rather than having NOTHING or ALL. I think we really did have our Great Adventure after all!"

Marajeane Zodtner

Marajeane Zodtner is a great grandmother who loves fun stories with deeper messages. The idea for this book—her first book ever—came to her in a flash in the wee hours of a summer morning. Marajeane was born in Wisconsin and lived in both California and Michigan for many years before ending up in South Carolina. She enjoys retirement from her home on Hilton Head Island after many years as a Michigan school district Business Manager. She is an active member of her church's Social Services Committee and participates in the Lil-Pantry and Thursday Soup Kitchen. Marajeane likes to say, "My family is a happy and loving circle of children, grandchildren and great-grandchildren. This is my way of sharing with them what is really important as they go through life."

Madeleine Kunda

Madeleine Kunda is an award-winning illustrator, writer and graphic designer from Telluride, Colorado. Her work has been featured by MountainFilm, the Telluride Ski Patrol and the National Ski Areas Association. She is the illustrator of several children's books and films including *Lids on Kids*, *The Tails of Otis and Bear* and *The Unlikely Journey of Leo the Leaf*, which was named a 2020 Distinguished Favorite by the Independent Press Award. A linguist, PADI Instructor and EMT, Madeleine loves travel and the great outdoors.

CPSIA information can be obtained
at www.ICGtesting.com
Printed in the USA
LVHW071204300321
682935LV00015B/445

* 9 7 8 1 7 3 5 5 9 6 0 7 5 *